For Johann and Joseph

Copyright © 2006 by Annette Betz Verlag im Carl Ueberreuter, Vienna, Munich.
First published in Austria under the title *Wie Mama und Papa Verliebte wurden*.
English translation copyright © 2008 by North-South Books Inc.
All rights reserved. No part of this book may be reproduced or utilized in any
form or by any means, electronic or mechanical, including photocopying, recording, or any information
storage and retrieval system, without permission in writing from the publisher.
First published in the United States, Canada, Great Britain, Australia, and New Zealand in
2008 by North-South Books Inc., an imprint of NordSüd Verlag AG, Zürich, Switzerland.
Library of Congress Cataloging-in-Publication Data is available.
A CIP catalogue record for this book is available from The British Library.

ISBN: 978-0-7358-2176-7 (trade edition)
1 3 5 7 9 10 8 6 4 2

Printed in Belgium

www.northsouth.com

Published in cooperation with Annette Betz Verlag, Vienna, Munich.

How Mommy Met Daddy

Katharina Grossmann-Hensel

Translated by Rachel Ward

NORTHSOUTH BOOKS

NEW YORK / LONDON

A long, long time ago, before I was born, my parents were little, like me. But they were nothing at all alike!

Mommy liked things that were colorful and messy. Daddy liked everything plain and neat.

When Mommy got dressed in the morning, she'd yell, "Three, one, two!" and dive into the gigantic heap of clothes on her floor, crawling through it until enough things stuck.

Daddy numbered the shelves in his bookcase from one to ten. Everything had its own shelf. His idea of an exciting afternoon was switching the stuffed cow on shelf nine with his paper and pencils on shelf four!

When Mommy and Daddy were all grown up, they moved to the city and they each opened a store.

Daddy only sold things that were black and white, and his store was very tidy. People would come in and buy shoe polish or soap.

'It's a bit dreary in here,' they thought, and they never went back. Daddy's store wasn't very busy.

At her store, Mommy sold colorful clothes that she made herself. But her store was so messy that people thought it was a garbage heap, and they rarely even came in!

Winter was too dull for Mommy, and she would sit in the window and wait for Spring to come with all its colors. 'Oh, it would be lovely to have someone who'd dance like mad with me, and mess everything up!' she thought.

Summer was too bright and colorful for Daddy. He would jump from one shady spot to the next. 'Oh, it would be lovely to have someone who would stay inside with me,' he thought.

Mommy and Daddy were lonely. At night they would both look up into the sky. 'Isn't there anyone out there who's just like me?' they wondered.

Then one day, Daddy was walking down the street, trying not to step on any cracks in the sidewalk. At the same time, Mommy, who was late as usual, was running along from the other direction, not watching where she was going. Then they both came to the corner and . . . **CRASH!**

They held their heads and saw each other for the first time. Daddy went a bit red and Mommy went a bit white.

"Are you alright?" Daddy asked.

"I'm fine . . . but I could really use a cup of coffee!" Mommy cried.

And so they went for coffee ...

"That's a pretty dress," Daddy said once they were seated, which was funny, because Mommy's colorful dress wasn't at all to his taste.

"And your white coat is very handsome," said Mommy. Which was strange, since it was perfectly ironed and spotless.

Mommy felt like she had butterflies in her tummy, and Daddy's heart was beating so hard, it almost shook the table. 'Must be the coffee,' they thought.

Daddy danced down the sidewalk the whole way home. That evening, instead of folding his pants and putting them on the chair as usual, he just threw them in a heap on the floor.

That night he dreamt of a colorful dress. In the morning, he had no idea what he was supposed to do. Daddy had forgotten everything—there was only room in his head for bright clothes.

'What's the matter with me?' he wondered.

Mommy soon realized that there was something wrong with her, too. In the morning she sewed hearts on all of her clothes. In the afternoon she made heart-shaped shopping bags, and in the evening she made a white coat.

'What's happening to me?' she wondered, tidying up her shop for the first time ever.

Mommy felt a little sick and she couldn't eat. Daddy felt like there was a big hole in his stomach. 'I'm missing something,' they both thought. 'But what—or *who*—could it be?'

The next day, Daddy buried his red face in his hands. "I must be ill!" he groaned, jumping out of bed and sliding down the banister. Then he skipped all the way to the doctor's office.

And who was sitting in the waiting room when Daddy arrived? Mommy! She was quite pale!

The Doctor came in and they both started talking at once. "We've got a contagious disease!" Daddy explained. "Suddenly I'm colorful and messy!"

"And I'm turning black and white and tidy!" said Mommy. "We've both caught a dangerous, contagious virus!"

"How long have you been feeling like this?" asked the doctor.

Mommy looked at Daddy, and her pulse started to race.

"Since we crashed into each other!" they answered together.
Daddy looked at Mommy and his heart started to pound.

"I see," said the doctor, who was watching them beam at each other.
"And has your condition changed in any way?"

"I started feeling a lot better in the waiting room . . ." mused
Mommy.

" . . . and the hole in my stomach disappeared when I got here!"
said Daddy.

"Well!" cried the doctor. "I prescribe lots of time together and
plenty of fresh air. You'll feel better in no time."

So Mommy and Daddy decided to work together till they were feeling like themselves again. Mommy helped Daddy reorganize his store. She hung her clothes on the white walls while Daddy put away the heart-shaped shopping bags. Daddy's face got red when his hand accidentally touched Mommy's, but he'd never felt better.

When Daddy was next to Mommy arranging tin cans, she felt silly and things slipped right out of her hands, but she was in the very best of moods.

At the grand opening of their new store, Daddy played the piano. Sometimes he played the white keys, sometimes the black keys, and sometimes he played with his feet!

Mommy spent the whole time at the cash register because they had so many customers. By evening they had sold everything in the store.

They stood in the empty shop, waiting for the virus to finally disappear and everything to return to the way it used to be.

But nothing happened.

As they walked through the parking lot, Mommy felt so light she thought she was floating. Then Daddy began floating too. "What's happening?" he cried.

A pink cloud drifted towards them.

"Of course!" Mommy said, clapping her hands as she pulled Daddy onto the cloud. "I know what's wrong with us!" and she gave him a big kiss. Now Daddy understood too.

"We're in love!"

"What? But how did you know?" I ask them now, "*Why* did you fall in love?"
Mommy and Daddy just smile at each other.
One day I'll find someone to fall in love with, but we will be just alike.
I'm sure of it.